PEANUTS

You're a Big Brother, CHARLIE BROWN!

By Charles M. Schulz
Adapted by Jason Cooper
Illustrated by Scott Jeralds

SIMON SPOTLIGHT
New York London Toronto Sydney New Delhi

SIMON SPOTLIGHT
An imprint of Simon & Schuster Children's Publishing Division
1230 Avenue of the Americas, New York, New York 10020
This Simon Spotlight edition February 2018
© 2018 Peanuts Worldwide LLC
For information about special discounts for bulk purchases, please contact Simon & Schuster
Special Sales at 1-866-506-1949 or business@simonandschuster.com.
Manufactured in the United States of America 0119 LAK
10 9 8 7 6 5 4 3
ISBN 978-1-5344-0961-3
ISBN 978-1-5344-0962-0 (eBook)

Sally cries a lot, but Charlie Brown doesn't mind.

After all, when she was born, Charlie Brown was so happy he couldn't think straight. He ran out the front door and down the street, announcing the good news to everyone.

"Guess what?" he shouted excitedly. "I'm a father! I mean, my *dad's* a father! Again! I'm a *brother*! I have a baby sister!"

DEAR PENCIL PAL,
    I'M SURE YOU'VE NOTICED IT'S BEEN A LONG TIME SINCE I HAVE WRITTEN TO YOU. AT LEAST I HOPE YOU'VE NOTICED. WELL, I HAVE SOME EXCITING NEWS. I HAVE A NEW BABY SISTER! HER NAME IS SALLY. . . .

Before Charlie Brown can finish the letter, he is interrupted by the sound of Sally crying.

He ran right past his friends Linus and Lucy.
"You weren't that excited when *I* was born," Linus complained to Lucy, his big sister. Lucy didn't deny it.

The first few weeks after Sally was born were some of the greatest times in Charlie Brown's life, partly because his friends were so happy for him and kept congratulating him.

"I tell you, Linus," Charlie Brown said, "people have not treated me so nicely since"—he stopped to think for a moment—"people have *never* treated me so nicely!"

Charlie Brown's dog, Snoopy, was excited about baby Sally too (and he was usually only excited when his supper dish was getting filled up). But even Snoopy sometimes wondered *why* he liked Sally so much. Sure, she liked to scratch behind his ears, but there was something else. He couldn't put his paw on it.

Then he saw Sally crawling. *That's it!* thought Snoopy. *She's the only other one around here who knows how to walk on four feet!*

Nowadays, Charlie Brown and Snoopy can't imagine life before Sally was part of the family.

Charlie Brown decides to take a break from writing his letter and talk with Lucy about siblings.

"No matter what happens," he tells Lucy, "Sally and I are family. I will always be there for her and she will always be there for me. That's a nice feeling."

Lucy chuckles. "Go ahead and tell yourself that, Charlie Brown. But trust me, your life is going to get worse. A lot worse."

Lucy's comments make Charlie Brown nervous.

"What do you mean?" he asks.

"You'll see," Lucy says. "You're going to have to share everything from now on. Food. Presents. Even your parents' love!" Lucy says.

"I like to share," Charlie Brown tells her.

Lucy looks at him closely. "Who do you think your parents are going to dote on more? A cute new baby . . . or old, wishy-washy you?"

Charlie Brown tries not to think about what Lucy said. Instead, he decides to finish the letter.

SOME FOLKS SAY THAT YOUR LIFE CHANGES A LOT WHEN YOU GET A NEW BROTHER OR SISTER. BUT I THINK . . .

But again, Sally starts crying. She is hungry and needs a bottle. Charlie Brown puts his pencil down.

"All right, all right," he calls out. "I hear you." He gets up and walks toward the kitchen to make a bottle . . . but he trips over Sally's blocks. "Good grief, Sally!" Charlie Brown yells. "Pick up your toys! I nearly broke my neck!"

Charlie Brown immediately feels bad about raising his voice.

"Sorry about that, Sally," he says. "You know what always calms me down? Working on a puzzle!"

Charlie Brown gets Sally her bottle, and then he finds his favorite jigsaw puzzle. Before he can snap the last piece into place, Sally crawls over the puzzle and messes it up!

Charlie Brown loses his temper again. "Sally! You ruined it!"

Sally cries even more!

Then Charlie Brown remembers that she is just a baby. She probably doesn't know why he is upset. Now Charlie Brown feels horrible.

"I'm so sorry, Sally," he says, and he gives her a hug.

Charlie Brown needs some air, so he meets up with Linus. "I feel terrible about yelling at Sally," he says.

"Don't feel too bad, Charlie Brown," says Linus, looking up from a comic book he is reading. "You made a mistake. It happens. But eventually you'll see that brothers and sisters can get along very well together."

Just then Lucy storms over and says to Linus, "That's *my* comic book!" She snatches it out of his hands and marches off.

Linus shrugs and starts to walk home. "See you at the game tomorrow!" he tells Charlie Brown.

Charlie Brown had forgotten all about the baseball game. Just thinking about it makes him feel better!

At home, Charlie Brown wonders if Sally will become as big a baseball fan as him.

Then he notices what Sally did—she had built a huge tower of blocks and trapped Snoopy inside it. As he frees Snoopy, Charlie Brown wonders what other surprises his sister will have in store for them.

The next morning, Charlie Brown tries, again, to finish the letter.

TODAY WILL BE SALLY'S VERY FIRST BASEBALL GAME! AND I CAN'T WAIT FOR . . .

And, again, he has to stop. This time, it's because his mom needs him to help with Sally . . . which means he won't be able to play baseball! Charlie Brown is crushed.

Charlie Brown pushes Sally's stroller to the baseball field.

"Charlie Brown! Where have you been?" Linus asks. "The game is about to start!"

Charlie Brown tells the team he won't be able to play.

"That's terrible!" cries Lucy. "You're our manager! How are we supposed to go out there and lose without you?"

Charlie Brown tries to help them. "Be sure to have the infield move in; try to cut off the run at the plate," he says, and he walks away.

"Poor guy," Linus says to Schroeder. "We really should try to win today for Charlie Brown."

Schroeder agrees. "Or in the very least, embarrass ourselves a little less than usual."

Charlie Brown is upset. "I know you can't help it, Sally," he grumbles, "but your timing is terrible."

Sally giggles, points at the clouds, and squeals. "Ducky!"

Charlie Brown smiles. He can't stay mad at her for long. In the end, they have fun playing together.

After the game, Linus stops by Charlie Brown's house.
"I'm glad you're feeling better, Charlie Brown," Linus says,
and he hands him a baseball. "It's the game ball. We actually
won today! I thought you'd like to have it."
Charlie Brown can barely speak. "Thank you," he whispers.

"I can't stand it, Sally!" Charlie Brown confesses when Linus leaves. "They won! My team doesn't need me at all."

Sally crawls toward him, holding a puzzle piece.

Charlie Brown smiles. "You know, Sally, it's not always easy, but if you and I stick together, we just might lick this ol' world yet. . . ."

That evening, while Snoopy teaches Sally some new dance moves, Charlie Brown finally gets around to finishing the letter.

... AS I WAS SAYING, PENCIL PAL, BEING A BIG BROTHER IS NOTHING LIKE I EXPECTED. IT IS EVEN BETTER!

YOUR FRIEND,
CHARLIE BROWN

TIERRA
VERDE
BIBLIOTECA DE
DESCUBRIMIENTOS

¿Te gustan las ciencias? ¿Quieres ayudar a cuidar la Tierra? Entonces, los libros de *Green Earth Science* son para ti. Cada libro te ayudará a descubrir cosas simples que puedes hacer para ser un amigo de la Tierra y a entender la evidencia científica que respalda el porqué esto es importante.

Para encontrar otros libros tan interesantes como estos, visite:
www.rourkeeducationalmedia.com

ISBN 978-1-6271-7398-8

90000

9 781627 173988

Printed in China

Rourke
Educational Media
rourkeeducationalmedia.com